Rosie

the cow who wanted to slim

Christel Desmoinaux

CAT'S Whiskers

THE WATTS PUBLISHING GROUP LTD

Farmer Jules was very proud of Rosie.
She was the most beautiful cow in the county.
She had a large round tummy,
and plump pink udders.

Rosie

the cow who wanted to slim

This edition first published in 2002 by
Cat's Whiskers
96 Leonard Street
London EC2A 4XD

Cat's Whiskers Australia
56 O'Riordan Street
Alexandria
NSW 2015

ISBN 1 903012 48 1 (hardback)
ISBN 1 903012 49 X (paperback)

A CIP catalogue record for this book is available
from the British Library

Printed in Hong Kong

Every day Rosie gave
Farmer Jules a whole churn
of creamy milk. He drank
a large glass in the morning,
and used the milk to make
delicious cakes for tea.

Tender grass

Fresh grass

Juicy grass

Sweet hay

Rosie had a wonderful life.
During the day she grazed on sweet, tender grass;
and in the evenings, she always chose
which TV programme they would watch.
Farmer Jules even bought her
'Moo Monthly'; it was her
favourite magazine.

Rosie loved Farmer Jules and Farmer Jules
loved his cow. Every day, at sunset,
he watched Rosie frolicking in the field.
Life was good!

One day, as Rosie turned the pages of
'Moo Monthly', she had a thought:
"Since I'm so beautiful, perhaps my photo
could go in the magazine..."

She looked at herself from all angles,
turned around and around, then groaned:
"But I'm much too fat! I'll have to go on a diet."

The next morning, when Farmer Jules brought sweet hay
for Rosie's breakfast, she turned away and said firmly:
"No thank you, I'm on a diet."
Later on, outside in the field, Rosie sat down
and refused to eat a single blade of grass.
Farmer Jules was worried.

To help her lose weight, Rosie started doing keep-fit.
For three hours each day, she jumped and pumped
and sweated. The other animals couldn't stop laughing.

Next, Rosie went to the chemist's.
She came away with lots of diet foods,
as well as a special cow-weighing machine.
Now, instead of grass,
she only ate
funny-tasting
soups!

Farmer Jules was very worried
about Rosie's health.
He tried talking to her.

But Rosie wouldn't listen.

Farmer Jules was in despair.

The worst thing was that his daily glass of milk
now came from cows he didn't know:

all Rosie could produce was a tiny drop of skimmed milk.

And there were no more cakes at tea-time.

1000 kg

700 kg

400 kg

Rosie, on the other hand, was very pleased with herself.
Little by little she had become an extremely slim cow!
She waited in the field patiently,
hoping that a fashion photographer
would spot her.

Farmer Jules retired to his bed.

One day Rosie saw two men looking at her.
She was sure they worked for 'Moo Monthly'.
"It's so sad!" the first man whispered.
"She used to be such a beautiful cow."
"Yes," said the other. "Now she looks more like
a giraffe without a neck!"
And they both laughed as they walked away.

"So sad? A giraffe without a neck?"
Rosie was puzzled. She went to look at
herself in the pond. "Oh my goodness!" she exclaimed,
"Is that poor skinny thing really me?"

Rosie suddenly felt very sad, remembering her lovely round tummy and her plump pink udders. "What have I done!" She threw her diet equipment into the dustbin and crept back to the farm.

"Farmer Jules, Farmer Jules!" she called softly. "I'm so sorry. I want to be how I was before - a beautiful plump cow!" Farmer Jules leapt straightaway from his bed and went to find her some hay.

And while Rosie ate and ate,
Farmer Jules was so happy
that he turned
cartwheels in the air.

Today Rosie is again the most beautiful cow in the county.
She knows she looks fine just the way she is!